Destiny's Gift

by Natasha Anastasia Tarpley

illustrated by Adjoa J. Burrowes

Lee & Low Books Inc. • *New York*

Special thanks to Angeli Rasbury of Nkiru Books in Brooklyn, New York,
and Brother Yao of Karibu Books in Hyattsville, Maryland,
for their help in the research of this story.
—N.A.T.

Text copyright © 2004 by Natasha Anastasia Tarpley
Illustrations copyright © 2004 by Adjoa J. Burrowes

Manufactured in China

Book design by David Neuhaus/NeuStudio
Book production by The Kids at Our House

The text is set in Prosperall
The illustrations are rendered in cut-paper collage, watercolor, and acrylic

10 9 8 7 6 5 4 3 2 1
First Edition

Library of Congress Cataloging-in-Publication Data
Tarpley, Natasha.
Destiny's gift / by Natasha Anastasia Tarpley ; illustrated by Adjoa J. Burrowes.— 1st ed.
p. cm.
Summary: Destiny's favorite place in the world is Mrs. Wade's bookstore, so when
she finds out it may close she stirs the community to help out, then works on a
special gift of her own to encourage Mrs. Wade.
ISBN 1-58430-156-2
[1. Bookstores—Fiction. 2. Community life—Fiction. 3. African Americans—Fiction.]
I. Burrowes, Adjoa J., ill. II. Title.
PZ7.T176De 2004
[E]—dc21   2003008894

*T*o all the Book People everywhere: librarians, teachers, parents, writers, readers, friends.
For opening up the chambers of my heart and imagination through books,
I am forever grateful. —N.A.T.

*T*o my sister, Cynthia Bowen, a loving source of strength and inspiration. —A.J.B.

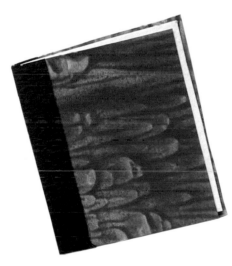

My favorite place in the world was Mrs. Wade's bookstore, across the street from my house. Mrs. Wade knew everything there was to know about words, and I loved words!

I went over to Mrs. Wade's every Tuesday and Saturday. As soon as I walked into the store, the wind chimes above the door tinkled a special hello.

"Hey there, Destiny!" Mrs. Wade would call out, and stop whatever she was doing to give me a big hug. She smelled like flowers and peppermint and had long, silver dreadlocks that fell to her waist.

"What's the word?" Mrs. Wade would ask.

"Let's go find out," I would say.

We'd rush over to the big, thick dictionary Mrs. Wade kept on a pedestal in the store. I'd close my eyes, open the dictionary, and point.

Whatever word my finger landed on was our word for the day. Mrs. Wade always helped me with words I didn't understand. We sounded out each word and picked it apart like a puzzle, until I knew all there was to know about the word.

I wrote down everything in my notebook, which I carried everywhere I went.

When I wasn't writing words, I was reading them—gobbling them up from the pages of books as if they were candy. Mrs. Wade always gave me new books to read. She even introduced me to real authors who came to read their books at her store. I liked to talk to them because they loved words just like I did.

That's how I decided I wanted to become a writer when I grew up.

On Saturdays Mama and Daddy let me stay at Mrs. Wade's until closing. I helped Mrs. Wade around the store. I watered the plants and fluffed the big, comfy pillows where people could curl up and read on the floor.

Then Mrs. Wade and I would put the new books on the shelves. Sometimes I'd open a book, stick my nose in between the pages, and take a big whiff. It smelled like ink and grass and the old clothes in my granny's closet. The crisp paper felt like autumn leaves between my fingers.

The part I liked best about these Saturdays was the end of the day, after all the customers had gone. Mrs. Wade would set up a tray with peppermint tea and butter cookies, the kind with a hole in the middle. We would drink our tea and pretend the butter cookies were diamond rings around our fingers.

Then I would read to Mrs. Wade from my notebook. She'd listen to my stories and poems with her eyes closed. I'd imagine I was a famous author, reading to a room full of people. Sometimes, after I finished reading, Mrs. Wade would open her eyes and say, "Words are a very powerful gift."

I wasn't sure what she meant, but I felt very important indeed!

Then one Saturday everything was different when I got to Mrs. Wade's store. Instead of talking to her customers or unpacking new books as usual, Mrs. Wade was reading a letter and looking very sad. She put away the letter and smiled when she saw me, but I could tell she wasn't her usual cheerful self.

Later, while we had our tea, Mrs. Wade told me what was wrong. She took my hands in hers, and we sat with our knees touching.

"Have you ever had a really tough assignment in school, but no matter how hard you try you just can't seem to figure it out?" she asked.

I nodded. Math problems were always like that for me.

"Well, I've been trying for a long time to figure out a way to keep the bookstore open, but I haven't had much luck," Mrs. Wade said, sighing. "My landlord is raising my rent, and I can't afford to pay the new amount. I may have to close the store." Mrs. Wade sighed again, and I thought I saw a small tear in the corner of her eye.

My heart froze midbeat. Close? No! I couldn't believe it.

"Why? Why do you have to close the store?" I asked, my voice shaking.

"I need to earn more money in order to pay the higher rent, and there just aren't enough customers for that," Mrs. Wade said.

"We can get more!" I shouted.

"We'll see." Mrs. Wade smiled a sad smile. "We'll see."

When I got home, I told Mama and Daddy about Mrs. Wade's store. I cried so hard, I didn't think I'd ever stop.

Mama and Daddy wrapped me in their arms.

"I know how much the store means to you," Mama said, stroking my hair.

"Maybe there's something we can do to help," said Daddy.
Mama and Daddy got on the telephone and called all our neighbors. The next day everybody on our block came to our house to talk about what we could do to save Mrs. Wade's store.

The following Saturday, all the kids in the neighborhood passed out fliers to get folks to come to Mrs. Wade's bookstore. The grown-ups contacted the local TV news stations and newspapers and called Mrs. Wade's landlord to ask him to lower her rent so the store could stay open.

On Sunday we made signs that said "Save Our Store" and then marched around the neighborhood. It felt like being in a parade.

The next Saturday we had a huge block party to raise money. There was singing and dancing and tables full of good food. I helped Mrs. Wade at her table, and we sold boxes and boxes of books.

I had so much fun, I almost forgot to feel sad. Almost.

Even with all the signs and the fliers and the block party, I still wanted to do something special for Mrs. Wade. I wanted to give her a gift that would be just from me.

I thought and thought, but couldn't come up with any ideas.

"What're you thinking so hard about?" Mama asked.

"I want to make a special gift for Mrs. Wade, but I can't think of anything," I said.

"Well, why don't you close your eyes and take a deep breath," Mama said. "Then remember all the good times you had with Mrs. Wade at the bookstore. I'm sure you'll come up with something."

I closed my eyes and followed Mama's suggestion. Suddenly I had an idea! I jumped up, got out a new notebook, and started to write.

I wrote down everything I loved about Mrs. Wade's store, from the sound of the wind chimes hanging on the door to the smell of the brand-new books and Mrs. Wade's peppermint tea.

I wrote all afternoon and all evening long. Mama and Daddy even let me write during dinner.

The next morning I finished writing and ran over to Mrs. Wade's store at its usual opening time. But when I got there, the store was closed!

My heart pounded with fear as I peeked through the front window. Could Mrs. Wade have closed the store without telling me?

I was about to go home to tell Mama and Daddy when I heard Mrs. Wade's voice.

"Destiny, here I am!" Mrs. Wade called from her stoop next door.

"Why isn't the store open?" I asked.

"I just needed some time to think," Mrs. Wade said.

"Will you have to close the store forever?" I whispered.

"I hope not, but I'm just not sure, Destiny," Mrs. Wade said sadly. "It's hard to know if customers will keep coming back."

I didn't know what to say. Then I remembered my notebook.

"I have a present for you," I said and handed the notebook to Mrs. Wade. Her eyes lit up with surprise when she opened it and saw: "Mrs. Wade's Bookstore, by Destiny Crawford."

"Why don't you read it to me?" Mrs. Wade asked, a big smile spreading across her face.

I read every word as Mrs. Wade listened with her eyes closed.

When I finished, Mrs. Wade gave me a big, long hug.

"Destiny, this is the best present anyone has ever given me," she said, beaming. "Words are a powerful gift indeed."

That time I knew exactly what she meant.

Mrs. Wade and I don't know if the store will close, but until then we are going to keep reading and writing and gobbling up all the words we can!

Once Around the Sun

POEMS BY

Bobbi Katz

ILLUSTRATED BY

LeUyen Pham

Harcourt, Inc.
Orlando   Austin   New York
San Diego   Toronto   London

Once
Around
the Sun

MOBILE

SEATTLE PUBLIC LIBRARY

January

January is
when your sled hurries
  to the park after school
  and flurries you
    down
    the
      hill
       again
       and
       again
        until your nose is a dull cold pain
         and your big toe starts to complain
         about the hole in your sock
         and you begin to wish
         your sled would stop
         whispering
         "one more time"
         and once—
           just once—
           pull
           you
           back
           up
           that
           hill!

February

February is
when a frost-feathered windowpane
tells your fingernail
to carve the first letters of your name—
    and then to put a heart around them
with just enough space
             for someone else's initials
               below yours.

March

March is
when a cheerleader
no longer
        cartwheels
    inside your chest
because the forecast is
"SNOW"
        and
March is
when your hands begin to dream:
one hand dreams
about being a fist
        thumping
    into the soft leather cup
        of a baseball mitt;
two palms dream
about closing around a wooden bat;
and ten fingers dream
    about the pull of the wind
        as it catches a kite
            and carries it high in the sky
                and even higher!

April

April is
when the earth
parades in a green so brand-new
you can almost hear it playing a tune,
turning tight buds
of forsythia bushes
into tiny yellow trumpets,
waking the dozing daffodils.
And
  April is
    when your blue slicker
      collects beads
        of misty drizzle
and the walk to Grandma's house
      is a skip-splash-dance!
And
when you get there
Grandma
tells you how each spring
she falls in love with the world
all over again—
and you understand.

May

May is
when the sky unties
a secret song bag
early every morning,
and the birds fly out—
chirping
   chirring
      warbling
         trilling
      twittering
     tweet-tweet-tweeting—
sweetly caroling
their own spring songs.

June

June is
     when your math book
is completely lopsided:
         the pile of unfinished pages on the right
         is
         skinny
but you need to use your left hand to hold down
all the stuff you've already learned.
     And
     June is
       when the gentlest rustle
        of a leaf outside the window
can drown out your teacher's voice
  and
every word on the spelling test spells:

S-U-M-M-E-R V-A-C-A-T-I-O-N!

July

July is
when my friends and I
bottle slices of the sky—
barefoot,
holding Mason jars,
trapping tiny flickering stars.
July is
when the Milky Way
doesn't seem so far away
and I imagine
there might be
stars like ours
and kids
like me.

August

August is
when it's so hot
that even ants sweat
and the praying mantis
shuttles its rakes
along the whisker-rough stem
of a sunflower
that is trying to tickle
the sky.

September

September is
when yellow pencils
in brand-new eraser hats
bravely wait on perfect points—
ready to march across miles of lines
in empty notebooks—
and
September is
when a piece of chalk
skates across the board—
swirling and looping—
until it spells your new teacher's
name.

October

October is
when night guzzles up
the orange sherbet sunset
and sends the day
to bed
before supper
           and
October is
when jack-o'-lanterns
grin in the darkness
           and
           strange company crunches
across the rumple of dry leaves
to ring a doorbell.
October is
when you can be a ghost,
           a witch,
                a creature from outer space . . .
almost anything!
And the neighbors, fearing tricks,
           give you treats.

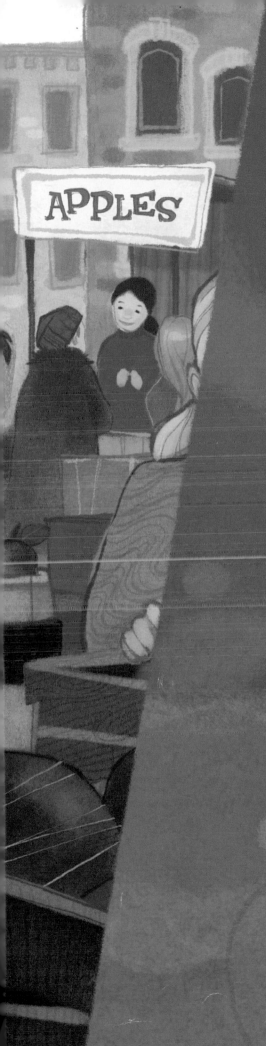

November

November is
when apples are not just apples
but families with names:
McIntosh,
    Northern Spy,
      Rome,
        Golden Delicious.
And November is
when cranberries are rubies,
sparkling pirate-booty
among the market bins
    full of chestnuts,
      turnips,
  bumpy yams. . . .
And
November is
when each pale turkey
silently waits to be chosen,
to be taken home and made wonderful again:
stuffed,
    roasted,
      carefully basted, until—
with a fanfare of smells—
it reappears in dark, crispy skin
to reign over Thanksgiving dinner!

December

December is
when greedy night
grows fat,
gnawing
   away the day
  until all that's left
of afternoon
is a small bare bone.
Finally,
the star-studded-sky-belly of night
gets too full for even one more bite.
At last, night's lost its appetite!
And
December is when
   just as
the shortest day
   is done,
who remembers Earth?
   The distant Sun!
Yes,
   the Sun remembers,
   turns back,
   and then. . .
Earth starts to *loop around it once again.*

For kids: with boundless affection!
Year after year after year, you keep me
connected to the wonder of each day
on our precious planet.
—B. K.

For the three new comets:
Vance, Kirk, and Darin Halverson
—L. P.

Text copyright © 2006 by Bobbi Katz
Illustrations copyright © 2006 by LeUyen Pham

www.HarcourtBooks.com

Library of Congress Cataloging-in-Publication Data
Katz, Bobbi.
Once around the sun/Bobbi Katz, illustrated by LeUyen Pham.
p. cm.
1. Months—Juvenile poetry. 2. Children's poetry, American.
I. Pham, LeUyen. II. Title.
PS3561.A7518O53 2006
811'.54—dc22   2004022500
ISBN-13: 978-0152-16397-6 ISBN-10: 0-15-216397-2

First edition
A C E G H F D B

The display type was set in Geetype.
The text type was set in Cantoria.
Color separations by Bright Arts Ltd., Hong Kong
Manufactured by South China Printing Company, Ltd., China
This book was printed on totally chlorine-free
Stora Enso Matte paper.
Production supervision by Pascha Gerlinger
Designed by Lydia D'moch

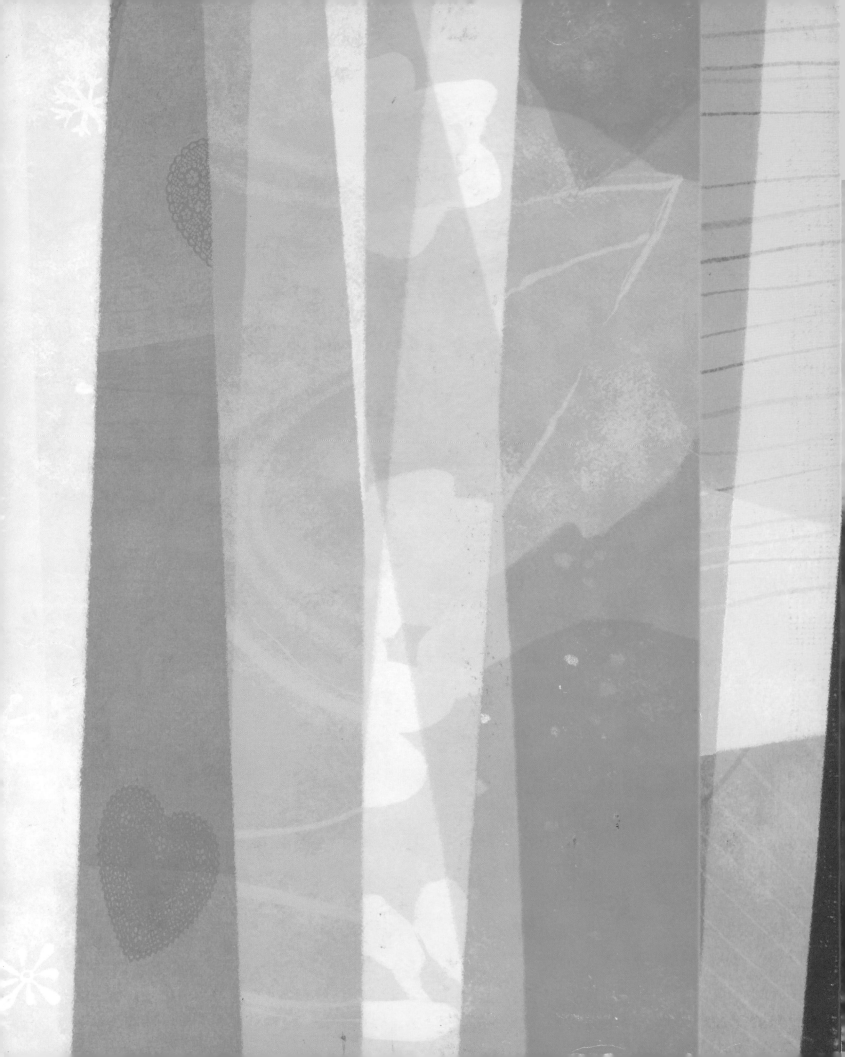